THE SCREAMING SKELETON

Look for these books in the
Clue™ series:

#1 WHO KILLED MR. BODDY?
#2 THE *SECRET* SECRET PASSAGE
#3 THE CASE OF THE INVISIBLE CAT
#4 MYSTERY AT THE MASKED BALL
#5 MIDNIGHT PHONE CALLS
#6 BOOBY-TRAPPED!
#7 THE PICTURE-PERFECT CRIME
#8 THE CLUE IN THE SHADOWS
#9 MYSTERY IN THE MOONLIGHT
#10 THE SCREAMING SKELETON

Clue™

THE SCREAMING SKELETON

Book created by A. E. Parker

Written by Marie Jacks

Based on characters from the Parker Brothers® game

A Creative Media Applications Production

SCHOLASTIC INC.
New York Toronto London Auckland Sydney

*Special thanks to: Diane Morris, Sandy Upham,
Susan Nash, Laura Millhollin, Chris Dupuis,
Maureen Taxter, Jean Feiwel, Ellie Berger,
Greg Holch, Dona Smith, Nancy Smith,
John Simko, Madalina Stefan,
David Tommasino, and Elizabeth Parisi*

ISBN 0-590-48936-4

12 11 10 9 8 7 6 5 4 3 2 1   5 6 7 8 9/9 0/0

Printed in the U.S.A.   40

First Scholastic printing, September 1995

To Matt

Contents

Allow Me to Introduce Myself . . .   1

1. Murder in the Cockpit   4
2. Baby Booty   16
3. Dance Until You Drop   25
4. The Halloween Costume Caper   35
5. The Snowball Effect   44
6. The Case Is All Sewed Up   53
7. Pie in Your Eye   63
8. Pea Is for Pretender   71
9. The Thanksgiving Murder   81
10. The Screaming Skeleton   89

THE SCREAMING SKELETON

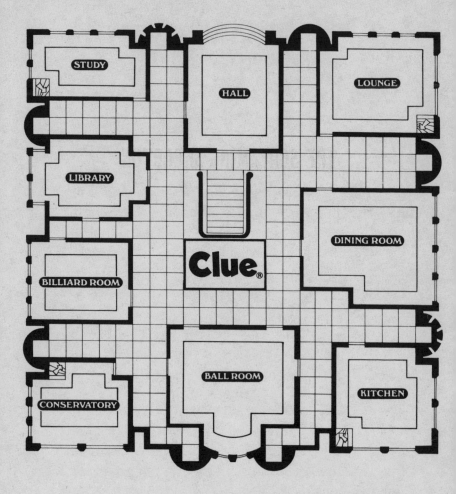

Allow Me to Introduce Myself . . .

My NAME IS REGINALD BODDY, AND I am your host for what promises to be another wild and woolly visit to my wonderful mansion. For those of you who have visited before, I extend a hearty "Welcome back!" For you new guests . . . well, prepare yourself for many, many surprises.

Sometimes my guests just don't know when to leave. Last visit, I had a deadly time of it getting them out of here. I even ended up with a stabbing pain in exchange for my effort. I suppose you might say one of my guests has a particularly "cutting" way of saying good-bye.

Fortunately, I quickly recovered and — against all reason — invited my regular guests back for another get-together. They were happy to oblige, though a few grumbled about having to check their weapons at the front door.

In a few moments I shall be joining them in the Library, where, no doubt, my guests are displaying their usual camaraderie and good cheer. That is, if they're not stealing me blind and plotting to kill one another. With your help, though, perhaps we all can make it through the visit in one piece.

Please allow me to introduce my suspects — I mean, my guests. There are six of them, including my loyal (if sometimes moody) maid, Mrs. White. (I will never be a suspect in any wrongdoing. You have my word on this, as a gentleman.) The six suspects you need to keep an eye (and, for that matter, an ear and a nose) on are:

Mr. Green: Many feel he will do anything to make a dollar. I may be mistaken, but I think I saw him delivering my newspaper this very morning. In any event, while he's happy with his own money, he wishes he had everyone else's, too.

Colonel Mustard: A sporting chap whose temper erupts quite easily. If he thinks someone has offended him, he will challenge him — or her — to a duel on the spot. Talk about a short fuse — one time he even offended himself!

Mrs. Peacock: A lady of painfully proper behavior. Rumor has it that her late husband was murdered because he failed to cover his mouth while sneezing. To this day, Mrs. Peacock denies having anything to do with her husband's death. After all, she says, a murderer displays very bad manners.

Professor Plum: He's softhearted — and equally softheaded. He considers everyone to be his friend, but only because he's forgotten who his enemies are. He signed up for a memory class. Unfortunately, he quickly forgot where and when it was to be.

Miss Scarlet: She doesn't consider herself vain — because she *knows* she's the world's greatest beauty. She *is* a rather pretty picture, it can't be denied. But I heard that when she travels, she buys two seats: one for herself, the other for her ego.

Mrs. White: This extraordinary servant has stood by me for years and years. Just make certain that she doesn't stand behind you with a Knife in her hands. She keeps the mansion shipshape — if you mean the *Titanic*.

There. A motley crew, I know.

Rest assured that at the end of each chapter, a list of rooms, suspects, and weapons will be provided so that you can keep track of the goings-on at the mansion this visit.

Well, it's time to fasten our seat belts. We're ready to take off and try to solve what I promise will be some very entertaining and challenging mysteries.

1.
Murder in the Cockpit

WHEN MR. BODDY'S GUESTS ARRIVED at the mansion, each was given a special invitation. The heavy envelopes were edged in gold and stamped with Mr. Boddy's special family seal.

"What's this about?" Mr. Green demanded. He tried to peel the gold edging off the envelope.

"Maybe Boddy's invited us to leave before we have a chance to unpack," said Miss Scarlet. She smelled the envelope to see if it was perfumed.

"How rude!" Mrs. Peacock said, glaring at Miss Scarlet. Always the lady, she took a silver-plated letter opener from her purse to gently open the invitation.

Professor Plum patted his pockets. "I'm afraid I forgot my glasses," he said. "Would someone be so kind as to read the invitation out loud?"

"Gladly," Colonel Mustard said, freeing his invitation. He cleared his throat and announced: " 'You are cordially invited to join me for a ride in my private jet. We will leave at dawn on Friday, and return at dusk the same day, following a stop in the south of France for a delectable lunch

4

and antique shopping. Your every comfort will be my pleasure. Signed, Mr. Boddy, your loyal friend and pilot.' "

"Boddy, a pilot?" Mrs. Peacock said. "Our host is a man of so many talents."

"Especially for being a millionaire," said Mr. Green.

"How rude!" stormed Mrs. Peacock. "You should never talk about money in polite company."

"Who said we were in polite company?" asked Mr. Green.

Doubly insulted, Mrs. Peacock took her invitation and left the room.

"Boddy being a pilot makes sense to me," Mrs. White said. "After all, he always has his head in the clouds!"

"When is this wonderful adventure?" asked Professor Plum, who had already forgotten.

"Friday," Colonel Mustard said. "At dawn."

"What will I wear?" mused Miss Scarlet. "I'll have to bring along one tiny suitcase to hold a change of outfits."

"One enormous trunk," muttered Mrs. White behind her fake smile.

"Personally, I love to fly," said Mr. Green. "That is, as long as I get my preferred seating."

Mustard nodded. "Flying can be awful if you're an aisle person forced to sit by the window."

"Or a window person forced to sit on the aisle," added Plum.

"Well, since I spend part of every day cleaning windows," Mrs. White said, "the last thing I want is a window seat when I fly."

"Never fear," said Miss Scarlet, bringing the conversation to a close. "Knowing Boddy, he will present us with the perfect seating arrangement."

At dawn on Friday . . .

At dawn on Friday, a very excited group met in Boddy's private hangar on the far grounds of his mansion. No one was more excited than Professor Plum, who was wearing swim goggles and a life preserver, and was carrying a rubber raft.

"Plum, have you lost your mind?" Green shouted.

"Think what you wish," Plum replied. "But *I'll* be ready in case Boddy's boat runs into any trouble."

"We're flying," Mrs. White whispered into Plum's ear. "In a jet."

"Ah, my mistake," said Plum, removing the aquatic gear.

Then the door to the jet opened and Boddy appeared. "Good morning," he told everyone. "A wonderful morning for flying. Rest assured that, with Mrs. White's help, I've — " He stopped short, eyeing the pile of luggage that Miss Scarlet had brought.

"Miss Scarlet, this is a private jet," Boddy said

sternly, "not a 747. Each passenger is allowed only one small carry-on bag."

"As is only proper," observed Mrs. Peacock.

While Miss Scarlet decided on what to bring, the other guests stepped into the shiny jet.

"I need to contact the air control tower," Boddy said. "Please help yourself to coffee, tea, milk, juice, regular soda, diet soda, or bottled water."

"Well, if we crash in the sea," Plum said, "no one will go thirsty."

"Look at these gorgeous leather seats," said Mr. Green, running his hand across the soft, brown seats.

"And all this lovely fruit," observed Mrs. Peacock, pointing to a tray of strawberries and melon.

"Oh, and smell the fresh coffee," inhaled Mustard as he helped himself to a cup from the silver pot. "I have to have several cups in the morning to be ready for any potential skirmishes."

"And all these newspapers and magazines!" said Mrs. White, thumbing through a recent edition of *Better Mansions and Gardens*.

When Scarlet finally boarded with a single bulging bag, Boddy sealed the jet door closed.

"Mr. Boddy, you are to be congratulated. I do believe you've thought of everything to make our trip enjoyable," concluded Mrs. Peacock. "You're a most wonderful host, indeed."

"Well," said Mr. Boddy, blushing slightly. "Thank you. But I have forgotten one thing."

"Earphones for the in-flight movie?" asked Mrs. White.

"The tiny bags of peanuts?" asked Professor Plum.

"The little plastic wings to pin on our collars?" teased Miss Scarlet.

"A map?" asked Mustard.

"Fuel?" asked Mr. Green.

"No," said Boddy. "I forgot to make a seating chart. Knowing all of you, there will be terrible arguments over who sits where."

"Don't be ridiculous," Scarlet told him. "We'll be happy to sit wherever you want us."

"Miss Scarlet is right," added Mrs. Peacock. "It's your jet. We're your guests. It's only right that you direct us to our seats."

"As you wish," Boddy said.

Boddy took out a diagram of the inside of the jet. "Let's see," he said. "We have two rows of three seats each, and a seat next to me."

"I'd be honored to sit in the copilot seat," offered Professor Plum.

Boddy noted the Professor's preference.

"I'd greatly prefer a window seat," insisted Mrs. Peacock. "Not on the left of the jet and not in the front row."

Boddy noted this, penciling in Mrs. Peacock's name.

"Well, I like the front row," said Mustard. "I

like to keep my eye on the pilot — no offense, Boddy."

"None taken," Boddy insisted, finding a seat for the Colonel.

"And I won't sit in his row," said Scarlet, moving away from Mustard. "I hate the smell of coffee. And I must have an empty seat next to me or I get horribly airsick."

"Yuck," whispered Mrs. White. "And if that happens, guess who gets to clean it up!"

"Yes," agreed Peacock. "Just the thought of airsickness is so very rude and distasteful."

"Let me see . . ." Boddy searched his seating chart. "Ah, here's the perfect seat for Scarlet."

"And I like the back row — close to the bathroom," admitted a sheepish Mr. Green. "Preferably in the middle."

"First airsickness, and now bathroom! Such talk!" shuddered Peacock.

"Just put me on the right side of the plane," added White. "If I'm on the left, or in the back row, I always get dizzy."

After trying various seating arrangements and then being forced to erase them, Boddy looked from his chart to his guests, shaking his head. "Ladies and gentlemen," he announced. "Trust that I shall do my very best to accommodate each and every one of you."

A few minutes later . . .

A few minutes later, Mr. Boddy finished his chart. "All right, then," he announced. "I believe I have it, now. It's full of eraser marks, but I think you can read it. Please take a look at this chart, and then take your seats. We must leave immediately. I believe I have accommodated every request — except for one."

"Except for one?" Scarlet repeated suspiciously. "Don't tell me, Mr. Boddy, that you're punishing me for overpacking!"

"You mean, I don't get to sit next to you," worried Plum with a tear in his eye.

"Please cooperate!" Boddy insisted, showing a rare display of temper. "We have been cleared for takeoff. If we don't leave instantly, I'll have to cancel the trip."

As Boddy situated himself in the cockpit and went through his final instrument check, the guests scrambled over one another to find their seats.

"Do you mind?" Peacock said as Mustard tried to take her seat first.

"Hey! I was here first!" stormed Mr. Green.

Mrs. White quickly strapped a seat belt over her lap. "Well, I for one am not budging!"

"May I see the chart again?" asked a puzzled Plum. "I forgot where I'm supposed to sit."

"Ouch! That was my foot you stepped on!" Mustard warned a pushy Miss Scarlet.

"Sit down!" Boddy ordered.

He began to taxi the jet down the runway.

The last of the guests took her seat. "The shopping in France had better be worth this bother!" she warned.

Cleared for takeoff, Boddy put his hand on the jet's throttle controls. Professor Plum, who was sitting next to him, was fascinated as he looked out the window of the cockpit. "This is so much fun," Plum said, "except for no peanuts."

"Prepare for takeoff," Boddy told his guests.

He was about to push the throttle forward — when a shot rang out!

The windshield of the plane exploded.

Glass flew everywhere.

The passengers braced themselves and screamed.

"Oh, dear!" a female guest cried.

"Boddy! Are you hurt?" Plum asked, attending to the pilot.

Boddy slumped over his instrument panel, and the plane came to a stop.

A guest jumped up from the back row. He was holding the Revolver. "That's what happens when I don't get to sit where I want!" he said, heading for the exit.

While the other guests looked on in horror, he

unsealed the jet door, jumped to the pavement below, and took off running.

WHAT WERE THE SEATING ARRANGEMENTS IN THE JET? AND WHO KILLED BODDY?

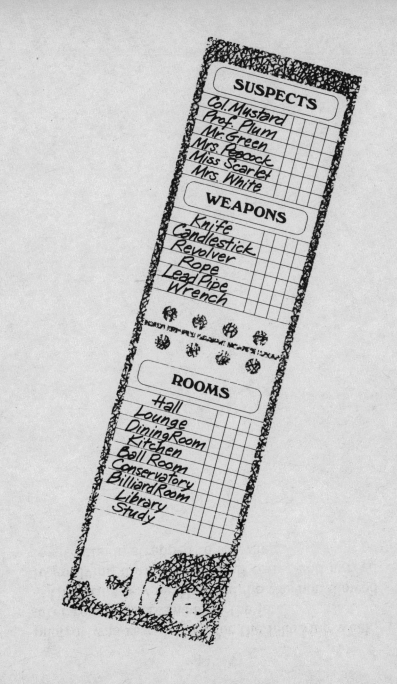

pilot, it was rescheduled for the following week, after repairs were made to the jet.

Unfortunately for Mustard, he was not allowed to go flying until he swore off coffee and agreed to sit outside strapped to the wing.

SOLUTION

COLONEL MUSTARD with the REVOLVER

The final seating arrangements were as follows:

	Boddy	Plum
Scarlet		White
Mustard	Green	Peacock

We know that every seating request but one was honored. And we know that the person whose request was not honored was the murderer. Further, we know the murderer was male and forced to sit in the back row.

Since Plum was up front in the copilot's seat, and Green wanted a seat in the back, the disgruntled and murderous guest can only be Mustard.

Honoring all of the rest of the original seating requests, we can then construct the final seating chart above.

Luckily, Boddy was not injured by the shot that shattered the cockpit window. He merely fainted from fright.

Though the trip had to be canceled by the dazed

2.
Baby Booty

ONE AFTERNOON, WHEN MR. BODDY and his guests were busy arguing over a game of charades in the Lounge, the doorbell to the mansion rang.

"I hope that's the pizza," Professor Plum said, rubbing his tummy.

"We didn't order any pizza," Mr. Boddy said. "Though it wouldn't be a bad idea."

"Pizza — how revolting," said Mrs. Peacock. "I refuse to eat any food that you pick up with your fingers."

"Good," said Mrs. White. "That will leave more pizza for the rest of us. I hope it's loaded with mushrooms."

"Well, I refuse to eat any food that grows in dark, wet caves," said Miss Scarlet. "Like mushrooms. The pizza had better be topped with pepperoni — or I'm going home!"

"But we didn't order any pizza," said Boddy, losing his temper.

The doorbell rang a second time.

"Then," Colonel Mustard told Boddy, "you'd

better tell the pizza delivery person that he or she has the wrong address."

"It's not a pizza!" shouted Mr. Boddy.

The doorbell rang a third time.

"All right, all right, I'll get it," Mrs. White said, finally getting up from her chair. "Even though my poor old legs are aching."

"Mrs. White, please stay put and you finish your game," Mr. Boddy said. "I'll answer the door myself."

"It worked again!" Mrs. White said to herself. She smiled with delight at her old trick.

In a few minutes, Boddy returned to his guests in the Lounge with a baby in his arms. The baby had bright-blue eyes and two big dimples. It was wrapped in a blue baby blanket.

Professor Plum scratched his head. "I wonder," he mused, "how that little, tiny baby reached the doorbell."

Mr. Boddy chuckled at his guests. "Please meet my nephew, Francis Boddy. He's my sister's child. We all call him Frank," said Boddy with obvious affection. "Don't you think he looks a bit like his old uncle Reggie?"

"A bit," said Miss Scarlet. "Right around the chin."

"He's the spitting image of his uncle," Green added. "Right down to the little bit of spit drooling off his lip."

"Be frank with us," Mrs. Peacock requested. "What is Frank doing here?"

17

Mr. Boddy explained, "I promised my dear sister that I'd watch the little fellow for an hour while she runs some errands. The nanny quit quite unexpectedly."

"Ah, that explains it," Plum said. "Your sister must have been tall enough to ring the bell. Well, now that that's settled, who's ready for another game of charades?"

At this, the baby made a sweet, gurgling sound.

Plum's eyebrows shot up. "Don't tell me the baby plays charades!"

"Probably better than you do," joked Mustard.

Boddy tickled his nephew under the chin. The baby smiled a toothless smile.

"Oh, he's absolutely adorable!" exclaimed Mrs. Peacock. She hurried over and took the baby from Boddy. "Oh, you sweet little oopsie-poopsie," she cooed.

"Oopsie-poopsie?" scoffed Mrs. White. "The woman's lost her mind."

"Keep the tot away from me," said Mr. Green. "Babies make me turn green."

"The problem with babies," added Miss Scarlet, "is that they're so small. Worse yet, they're too young to appreciate my beauty."

"Ah, and I'm too old," sighed Colonel Mustard.

"Nothing wrong with babies," said Professor Plum. "As long as I don't have to take care of them. Truth is, I don't remember how."

"Too bad," said Boddy. "I was going to offer each of you five hundred dollars to help me entertain the little guy for the next hour."

"Five hundred dollars?" said Miss Scarlet. She elbowed Peacock aside. "Why, come see your Aunty Scarlet, little oopsie-poopsie," she sang to baby Frank. "I'll let you play with my ruby bracelet — if you promise not to swallow it."

"I'll sing him a real lullaby," offered Mrs. White.

"I'll show him how to duel," offered Colonel Mustard.

"Dueling? For a baby?" protested Mrs. Peacock.

"My dear woman," Mustard replied, "it's never too early to show a tot the fine points of being a gentleman."

"I'll read to him," offered Professor Plum. "Something from Mother Goose, perhaps."

"Plum's a goose," muttered Mrs. White, reaching for the baby.

The guests surrounded Boddy and his nephew. Green made funny faces and ridiculous noises.

Then he began to recite, "The itsy-bitsy spider . . ."

Mrs. Peacock curled her nose up like a bunny and pretended she was eating a carrot.

Mrs. White crooned an old English lullaby while Miss Scarlet said, "Coochie, coochie, coo!" and tickled Frank under his little double chin.

19

Then, suddenly, the baby began to cry.

While the other guests stared in silence, Mrs. White took Frank to the Hall.

A few minutes later . . .

A few minutes later, the guests could still hear the baby crying in the Hall.

"Don't worry, I'll look into this," Colonel Mustard said. He went to the Hall to see what was happening with their young charge.

There, he saw Mrs. White struggling to quiet the unhappy tyke. "Can I help you, dear woman?" he asked.

"I think he's hungry," said Mrs. White.

"Hungry, you say," Mustard said. "I'm afraid I can't be of much help then."

"I'll just go to the kitchen and warm his bottle," Mrs. White said. "Here, you hold him and I'll be right back." With that, she gave baby Frank to an uncertain Colonel Mustard.

Not knowing what to do, Mustard tried bouncing the baby as he walked around the Hall. "Look here," he said, pointing to a portrait on the wall. "There's your great-grandfather. You look just like him. Especially the double chin."

This caused the baby to cry louder, so Mustard took him to the Study to look out the window. "Shhhh," he said, still bouncing up and down. "Shall I show you my swords, then?"

Just then, Miss Scarlet found Colonel Mustard and the baby. "Hand him over," she told Mustard. "I want to earn my five hundred dollars, too, you know."

Taking the baby, she held him close. "Why, you're cold," she said in a concerned voice. "I'm taking you to a warmer room, Frank. Soon, you'll be warmer and I'll be richer."

Scarlet carried the baby to the adjoining room, where she stood in front of the fireplace. But even the glowing fire didn't comfort Boddy's nephew.

"Wahh-wahh-wahh!" wailed the hungry baby.

Hearing the crying grow louder, Colonel Mustard went to the Kitchen to find Mrs. White and the much-needed baby bottle.

Then another guest found Miss Scarlet and the baby in front of the fire. "Let me try and hold him," the guest offered. "I think he smiled at me when I was doing 'Itsy-Bitsy Spider.' "

"I thought babies made you turn green," retorted Miss Scarlet. She pushed past the guest and out of the door. She carried Frank into the room between the northeast and southeast corner rooms of the mansion.

"Don't cry, Frank," Miss Scarlet pleaded. "I was a baby once, too. And it wasn't so bad. You'll grow out of it."

"You're still a baby," said an eager guest, also trying to earn the five hundred dollars. "And now it's my turn," said the guest.

"What do you think you can do that I haven't already tried?" said Miss Scarlet. "He needs his bottle, but we can't find Mrs. White."

"Look, I found a bell for him to shake," said the other guest. "That'll make him stop crying." She demonstrated, shaking the bell against the shoulder of her dress.

But the baby kept wailing. "Where is Mrs. White with his bottle?" demanded Miss Scarlet.

Just then, the other guest took Frank from Scarlet and whisked the crying child away.

Miss Scarlet just stood there and began to cry herself.

"I know just the place for you," the guest told him. "I'll take you to the room between the rooms in the southwest corner and the southeast corner of the mansion. That room has the most beautiful chandelier! It makes rainbows all over the walls when the sun shines."

WHO HAS THE BABY NOW?
WHAT ROOM DO THEY GO TO?
(*Hint*: Look at the diagram of the mansion opposite page 1.)

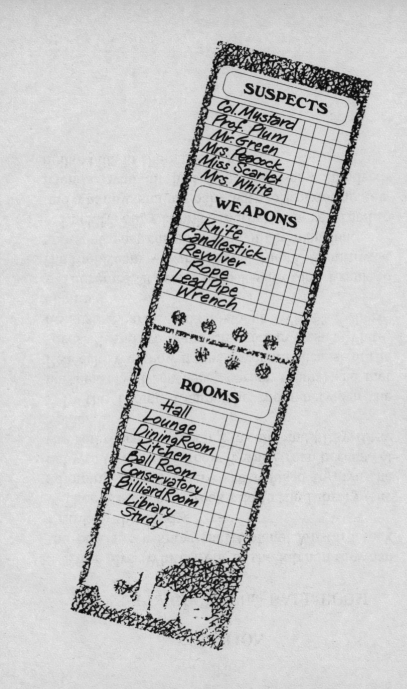

SOLUTION

MRS. PEACOCK in the BALL ROOM

After Mrs. White went to the kitchen to warm the bottle, we know that Colonel Mustard took Frank to the Study.

Then Miss Scarlet took him to the Library (the adjoining room), where she refused to give the baby to Green. We know it was Green because of the reference to "turning green" and "Itsy-Bitsy Spider."

In the Dining Room (the room between the northeast and southeast corner rooms) she met Peacock. We know it was a woman because of the "dress." And we know the woman wasn't White, because Scarlet asked about White's whereabouts.

Therefore, it was Peacock who took Frank to the Ball Room — which is between the southwest and southeast corner rooms of the mansion.

Luckily, baby Frank's mother soon returned to find a happy, smiling baby with lots of doting new friends, who all had five brand-new hundred-dollar bills in their pockets.

3.
Dance Until You Drop

Rainy WEATHER HAD FORCED MR. Boddy and his guests to cancel their planned croquet tournament. Colonel Mustard became so upset that he challenged his host to a duel.

"My good man," Boddy said calmly, "do you blame me for the storm?"

"Ah, a good point," said Mustard, backing off. "But it's a sticky wicket that the tournament was canceled. I've been practicing for months!"

"What you should practice is your manners," observed Mrs. Peacock. "Challenging our host to a duel — that's very bad form."

"Rain, rain, go away," sang Mrs. White sadly.

"Yes," said Mr. Green. "And I had a feeling I would have won the match today."

"By cheating!" said Miss Scarlet, taking off her wet shoes.

"No arguing!" said Mr. Boddy. "I have a wonderful idea. Follow me, please."

He led his guests into the Ball Room. Then he addressed the group.

"Listen, everyone. I've been taking dancing les-

25

sons," continued Mr. Boddy, "and I've gotten quite good. Would anyone care to tango?"

"Tangle?" asked Colonel Mustard, snapping to attention. "I'll tangle with anyone, man or beast!"

"It's a type of dance, you silly man," said Mrs. White. "From South America."

"Oh," said Colonel Mustard, putting down his sword. "You know, I used to take tap dancing lessons. It helps one be quick-footed in battle."

Mr. Green laughed at this. "And do you wear those shiny black shoes while you fight the battle?"

"Well, I prefer the waltz," said Mrs. Peacock. "It's a much more dignified type of dance than a tango."

"I'm fond of the fox-trot, myself," added Professor Plum. "Does anyone remember that fine old dance?"

No one replied.

Finally, Scarlet kidded the professor, "You probably don't remember yourself."

"My favorite dance is the cakewalk," boasted Mrs. White. "The favorite dance of all great cooks. Although there are a few chefs who prefer the mashed potato, I hear."

"I used to do the twist," admitted Mustard. "That is, until I twisted my lumbar something awful."

"I know what you mean," agreed Plum with a nod. "I was quite the spectacle at the local disco —

up till the moment that I ruptured a disk. Not surprisingly, after my injury, my disco phase quickly fizzled."

"I've learned all the most popular dances throughout the ages," said Boddy, doing a little two-step. "From the waltz to the twist to the hustle."

"No doubt it took you ages," said Scarlet, fingering her ruby necklace. "I like to rock around the clock, myself. Really shake my booty."

"Shake your what?" gasped a horrified Mrs. Peacock. "Why, of all — "

"She means the great dances of the nineteen fifties," explained Green. "I myself was known to trip the light fantastic."

"You're neither light nor fantastic," said Mrs. White with a wicked smile.

"Now, now, let's stop arguing," said Boddy. "Gather round, everyone, and I'll give you a demonstration."

A few minutes later . . .

A few minutes later, Boddy finished stacking old records onto an ancient record player.

"The first number," he announced, "is the tango."

As the slow, sizzling melody began, Mr. Boddy approached Mrs. Peacock. "Madam," he asked, "would you give me the pleasure of a tango?"

"Why, thank you, kind sir," replied a blushing Peacock. "But I told you, I prefer the waltz."

"Then let me cut in and waltz with you," said Mustard, bowing low to Peacock.

Mustard and Peacock waltzed across the Ball Room floor. They looked a little strange, waltzing to the sizzling tango tempo.

Then Professor Plum asked Mrs. White to dance.

"I can think of things I'd rather do," she replied. "Like dance with my feather duster."

"Go on, Mrs. White," urged Boddy. "It's fun!"

With a sigh, Mrs. White accepted Plum's offer, and they joined the other couple in the middle of the Ball Room floor.

"Plum, that was my foot you just stepped on," moaned Mrs. White.

"Gracious, I'm so sorry," said Plum. "Now would you mind moving that feather duster away from my nose?"

"Ladies and gentlemen, please pay attention," Boddy told the dancers, "while I demonstrate just a few of the many fancy steps I know."

"And how few steps he actually knows," sneered one of the dancing guests.

While Boddy danced by himself to the music, one of the dancing couples hatched a plan.

"Did you see Scarlet's necklace?" asked the woman.

"Yes," said the man. "Rubies. Dozens of them on a silver chain. Worth thousands."

"If somehow we got close enough to loosen the clasp . . ." the woman dancer began.

"One of us could grab it when it falls to the floor," her partner concluded.

They danced away, still plotting.

"I learned this move from watching a Fred Astaire movie," Boddy told the others, tapping both feet as fast as he could to the melody's beat.

"Well, everything he did, his female partner did backwards while wearing high heels," commented Miss Scarlet.

Then, Green, eyeing Scarlet's expensive necklace, approached her.

"Would you do me the favor?" he asked, bowing.

"Would you do me a favor and dance yourself out the front door?" Scarlet replied.

"Just one dance," begged Mr. Green, whisking her away as Professor Plum and Mrs. White passed by.

"If you step on my foot one more time, I'll see that you never walk — much less dance — again!" they heard Mrs. White grumble.

Finally, the first song ended. Boddy rushed over to the old phonograph and played with the buttons until the second record fell into place.

"All right, everyone," he shouted, "change partners."

Mr. Green and Colonel Mustard exchanged partners — until Mrs. Peacock asked for a breather. "I'm beginning to — well, glisten," she told her partner as she wiped her brow with a lace handkerchief.

"Ah, much better," sighed Mrs. White, pleased with her new partner.

When the third song came on, Scarlet's partner asked her for a second dance. "Don't push your luck," she said, retreating to a corner of the Ball Room.

There, she sank down into a chair and pulled out a compact. She checked her face for any trace of freckles.

Then a woman joined Scarlet and asked, "Did you know that the tag of your gown is sticking out in back?"

"Oh, no!" cried Miss Scarlet. "That's the sort of thing that a fashionable woman like me has nightmares about!"

"Here, I can just tuck that annoying tag back in place." The woman reached around to the back of Scarlet's neck.

Then a third woman came over and joined the other two. "Perhaps I can be of help," she offered. "We women have to stick together."

"I'm fine now," said Scarlet. "Just fine."

Then Boddy spotted the three women in the corner, and the men over in another corner. No one was dancing!

"I'll get everyone up and moving again," he told himself. He looked through the records, and finally found the one he wanted. "All right, everybody!" he shouted. "It's time to rock and roll!"

He cranked up the volume and rock and roll music blasted out of the speakers. The beat of the drum made the chandelier shake. The portrait of Boddy's great-great-great-uncle, Sir Reginald Arthur Charles Edward George Richard Boddy, crashed to the Ball Room floor.

"Finally," Scarlet said, standing up, "something I can dance to." She grabbed the guest who had tucked her tag in and began to boogie-woogie around the Ball Room.

"Let me go!" said Scarlet's partner.

"Too late!" laughed Miss Scarlet, dancing to the beat.

"Come on, baby," Mr. Green shouted. "Twist and shout!" He began to twist and shout — and everyone else gave him plenty of room.

Professor Plum got down on all fours and began turning somersaults in time to the music.

"Careful, Plum," Boddy warned. "Remember your bad disk!"

Colonel Mustard jumped up and down, waving his fists in the air. "Prepare for battle!" he shouted happily.

Even Mrs. Peacock did a little dance as she fanned herself in time to the beat.

"*Now* we're having a good time!" Boddy said

happily, looking around at all of his giddy guests. "You just have to find the right music to make a great party."

But all of a sudden, Miss Scarlet screamed. It was such a loud scream that it could be heard above the rock and roll. Holding her neck, she screamed again.

Mr. Boddy stopped the music. "What's the matter?" he asked. "Have you hurt yourself?"

"My necklace is gone," moaned Scarlet. "It's gone, and one — no, two of you are guilty!"

WHO STOLE MISS SCARLET'S NECKLACE?

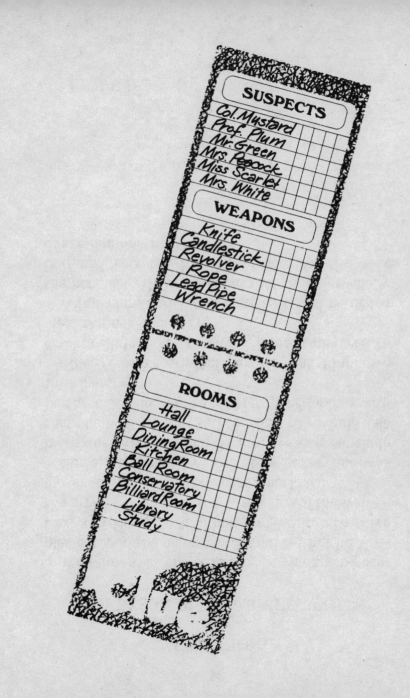

SOLUTION

PROFESSOR PLUM and MRS. WHITE

We know that one of the first two dancing couples hatched the plan, which would either be Mustard and Peacock, or Plum and White. To solve the mystery, we need to know which of the women loosened the clasp on Scarlet's necklace.

Since, at the end of the story, everyone was mentioned dancing but White, we can conclude that she was dancing with Scarlet. She would also be the one "closest" to Scarlet after fooling with the clasp.

Since White's original partner was Plum, we can conclude that the two of them conspired to steal the necklace.

After Plum and White confessed and returned the necklace, Boddy insisted that they personally buff and wax the Ball Room floor for the next dance demonstration.

4.
The Halloween
Costume Caper

IT WAS A WEEK BEFORE HALLOWEEN,
and Mr. Boddy was eager to celebrate.

"How I love Halloween," he mused. "A time to
scare everyone out of his or her wits — and get
sick eating gobs of trick-or-treat candy."

"Certainly sounds like a good time to me," said
Mrs. White, pretending to be interested.

"As a lad I loved helping my parents carve the
pumpkin," Boddy continued. "Nothing like sticking your hand into a pumpkin loaded with a zillion
slimy seeds."

"Nothing like it," echoed Mrs. White, rolling
her eyes.

"What should do we this year for Halloween?"
asked Boddy.

"We could turn off all the lights and pretend
we're not home," suggested Mrs. White.

"Oh, Mrs. White," chuckled Boddy, "you are
such a kidder!"

Mrs. White smiled so tightly, her ears ached.
"What do you wish to do for Halloween?" she
asked her employer.

"I know!" Boddy beamed. "How about a costume party?"

"For how many people?" asked Mrs. White.

"Oh, just all my usual guests," answered Boddy.

"What a wonderful idea," she told him. To herself she added, "What a terrible idea since I'll have to prepare all the food and drink."

Boddy snapped his fingers. "And I just had another idea!"

"I can't wait to hear it," Mrs. White said with her jaws clenched.

"We'll decorate the mansion to look like a haunted house," Boddy told her. "Cobwebs everywhere. Ghosts and skeletons and jack-o'-lanterns everywhere. Spooky music and sound effects. Can't you see it, Mrs. White?"

"Oh, yes, sir," she said with a fake smile. "And guess who gets to clean up afterwards," she muttered to herself.

The next week . . .

The next week was an incredibly busy time at the mansion.

Boddy and Mrs. White decorated every room from floor to ceiling.

They carved fifty jack-o'-lanterns.

Mrs. White baked dozens of cookies in the

36

shapes of pumpkins, witches' hats, broomsticks, and skulls.

The day of the party, Mrs. White and Boddy made spiced apple cider.

"I'm going to be a bat," Boddy declared proudly.

"Ah," said Mrs. White. "Well, I'm not giving you even a hint about my costume. You won't recognize me, I'm sure."

"Last year you went as me," Boddy reminded her.

"Yes," said Mrs. White. "I enjoyed being a billionaire for a night."

An hour before the party . . .

An hour before the party, Mr. Boddy inspected the mansion. "Excellent work," he said, complimenting Mrs. White. "I believe we have everything ready to go!"

"I'm ready to go to bed," she told him wearily.

"Go ahead and take the next half hour to yourself," he insisted. "You deserve it."

"Oh, thank you, kind sir," she said, stumbling toward her room.

Boddy went upstairs to his own room. There on the bed was a box from Cackling Cathy's Costume Consortium, which he opened. "Ah, it's perfect," said Boddy, admiring the wings of his bat costume.

As he changed into the costume, he wondered

how his guests would disguise themselves. "I bet Peacock will be dressed as a peacock, Plum as a plum, Green as a grape, Mustard as a jar of — " He stopped, shaking his head. "No. Not even my guests would be so obvious."

A half hour later . . .

A half hour later, the costumed guests made their way into the Ball Room. They disguised their voices so that they wouldn't be detected. They moved about the room, trying to find clues to guess who was who.

"Boddy has outdone himself this time," Colonel Mustard observed. "This place has become a first-rate haunted house."

"It's very, very spooky-looking," added a horrified Plum.

Mrs. Peacock pointed to the ceiling. "Either Mrs. White is a terrible housekeeper — or those cobwebs are frighteningly realistic," she said.

"Ah-ooo-oooo," moaned a scary voice, causing Mr. Green to jump into Miss Scarlet's arms.

"That was only a sound effect coming from a hidden speaker," Scarlet said, dropping Green to the ground. "Get hold of yourself, man!"

In the dim candlelight, the guests took note of the ghosts that seemed to fly through the air. (They were actually bedsheets on wires.)

But the most amazing thing was that no one could recognize anyone else.

"Welcome to Mystery Manor," croaked Boddy, making his entrance with a sweep of his bat wings.

"Has Boddy gone batty?" asked a guest.

"Help yourself to my homemade Bat Blood Punch and Cat Eye Cakes," the bat continued. "Dance the night away! And don't forget to bob for apples!"

"Bob for apples? That's a child's game," complained a guest dressed in a black cape and black hat.

"Oh, go take a few laps on your broom," remarked a character dressed in a black bodysuit and mask marked with glowing white paint.

"I wouldn't talk if I were you, you old bag of bones," said a creature with a green face and a large screw in his neck.

"What a monster you are," observed a ghost. "I'm green with envy over your costume."

"You're Green, all right," added a fat, orange pumpkin. "So you might as well give up the ghost and go home!"

"Watch it," said the ghost, "or I may have to carve you into a jack-o'-lantern."

"How rude!" snapped the pumpkin. "Have you no manners?"

"Aye, aye, mates!" said a feisty guest with tall black boots, an eye patch, and a sword. "Enough jabbering! Best behave or I'll make you walk the plank!"

"Ah, quiet yourself!" said the ghost. "You couldn't find your way home with a map marking the spot."

"Let's bob for apples, like the bat said," advised the guest wearing the eye patch. "I hear there's a gold nugget inside one of the apples. A sunken treasure!"

"That's right!" said the bat. "There is something gold and sweet inside one of those delicious red apples."

At this, the guests charged across the room to a big silver tub filled with water and bright-red apples.

"Me first, me first!" they screamed, pushing and elbowing their way to the tub.

Mrs. White jabbed the skeleton with her broom. "Move over, bonehead, or I'll use you to make soup," she said.

"Madam," interrupted a guest, "if you don't stop pushing, I'll have to challenge you to a duel."

White then poked that guest with her broom. "I think you have a screw loose," she told him. With that, she moved to the front of the line.

"Wait a moment," commanded the bat. "I won't have my party spoiled by all this arguing. And you'd better hurry. It's ten minutes before midnight. The winning apple must be bitten before midnight, or I may bite each of you!"

A few minutes later . . .

A few minutes later, the guests finally settled into a line.

"Very good," said the bat. "Now one at a time."

The first guest's face dove into the water. "Oh, that's cold!" Nevertheless, a second bob produced an apple.

The guests took turns bobbing until each guest had an apple. Dripping wet, they furiously chomped on their apples, eyeing each other with suspicion.

Then, after a few moments, a guest screamed out, "I have it! I have the gold nugget."

"I can't believe it," complained the disappointed witch. "The skeleton won! She pushed me aside and got the apple that should have been for me!"

WHO BIT THE GOLDEN APPLE?

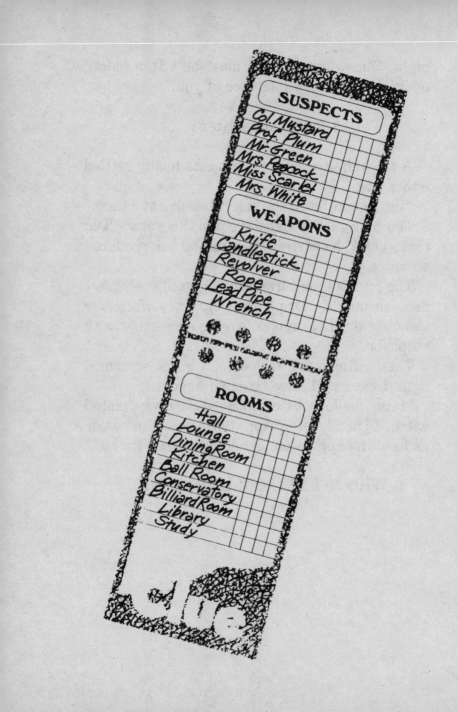

SOLUTION

MISS SCARLET is the winner.

We know that Green was the ghost and that Peacock was the pumpkin.

Later, we learned that White was the witch, when she poked the skeleton with her broom. The person who then interrupted was Mustard, because he challenged White to a duel. White then made a comment about his "loose screw" — which had to be a reference to Mustard's monster costume.

This left a pirate and a skeleton with unknown identities. When the skeleton won the apple bobbing, White called her a "she" — so we know it must be Scarlet. This makes Plum the mysterious pirate.

Though everyone was envious of Miss Scarlet at first, they had a good laugh when the bat announced with glee that the "gold nugget" was really a nugget of caramel candy.

5.
The Snowball Effect

ON A PARTICULARLY SNOWY DAY, when all the guests were inside whining like a room full of two-year-olds, Mr. Boddy had a winning idea.

"Let's go outside and play in the snow!" he suggested.

"Too cold," whined Miss Scarlet.

"Too deep," added Mr. Green.

"Too cloudy," said Colonel Mustard.

"I insist," said Boddy. "Some fresh air would do all of us a world of good."

The guests all groaned.

"Come on," Boddy said firmly. "Put on your warm coats, gloves, scarves, boots, and hats, and meet me outside."

"Coat, gloves, scarf, boots, and hat," repeated Scarlet. "I'm already exhausted."

"See you in five by the frozen fountain in the front flower garden," Boddy called as he left.

Five minutes later . . .

44

Five minutes later, the guests met Mr. Boddy by the fountain.

"Now what?" everyone asked.

"Let's have a snowball fight!" Boddy said enthusiastically. "It will be great fun."

"Phooey," said Mr. Green.

"How boring," said Miss Scarlet.

"I'd rather have a duel!" exclaimed Colonel Mustard.

"Is it too soon to go inside for a proper cup of hot, steaming tea?" asked Mrs. Peacock, moving her feet to stay warm.

"Someone, please decide," complained Professor Plum. "Before we all freeze to death!"

"Grrr!" said Mrs. White. "I mean, brrrr!"

"I'll give the winning team a prize," said Mr. Boddy.

Suddenly, everyone loved the idea.

"Winter is my favorite season," chirped Mrs. Peacock.

"The snow, it's so beautiful!" chimed Miss Scarlet.

"I feel better already," Plum added.

Boddy wrote each of their names on a slip of paper. He then put the slips in his hat.

"Draw names for teams," Boddy instructed.

The newly cooperative guests eagerly drew slips of paper from the hat.

"I'll act as referee," Boddy said. "And put these on, so you'll know who's on which team." He passed out three knitted green hats to one team and three knitted white hats to the other team. "This way you won't accidentally snowball your own team member," he explained.

"Personally, I would have preferred something in red," Scarlet said, putting on her hat.

"Oh, one last thing," Boddy said. "Everyone empty his or her pockets of weapons. I don't want any weapons but snowballs."

"Mr. Boddy," protested Mustard, "I'm offended that you think I'm carrying a weapon on my person." With that, Mustard stamped his foot in anger. Unfortunately for him, he stamped so hard that the Lead Pipe fell from his trouser pocket.

"Very well," Scarlet said, pulling the Revolver from her jacket and handing it to Boddy.

"All in the spirit of sportsmanship," Green added, handing over the Wrench.

"I'd give you the Rope," Plum said, "but it's holding up my pants."

"Mrs. White, go get the professor one of my belts," said Boddy, taking the Rope.

"Here, take the Knife," she said before rushing into the mansion and returning with a belt for Plum.

"Mrs. Peacock . . ." Boddy stared at her.

With a huff, she handed over the Candlestick. "I brought it outside in case we needed a fire to stay warm," she insisted.

"Of course," Boddy said. "Now, teams, go to your stations!"

The guests went off in two directions, so each team could make a snowy pile of "weapons."

"I'd much rather have the Wrench," commented Green. "The Wrench doesn't leave your hands wet and cold."

"Quiet, Green," said one of his teammates, "and keep packing more snowballs."

When both teams had assembled an ample supply of snowballs, Boddy called them all together.

"Here are the rules," he said. "If you are hit by a snowball, you must sit down."

"In the snow?" said a shocked Mrs. Peacock.

"In the snow," said Boddy with a nod. "The team with the last person standing wins. Ready?"

"Ready!" cried the eager guests, ducking behind their separate "forts."

Boddy blew his whistle and the teams cheered.

Immediately, snowballs began to fill the air.

Boddy ran for the cover of a large tree to watch the action.

"Take that!" Mustard shouted, lobbing a snowball like a hand grenade.

"And that!" Scarlet shouted, whipping one underhand like a bowling ball.

"Missed!" taunted Plum, sticking out his tongue.

"Wait a second," suggested Mr. Boddy, waving his hands. "Let's take it one team at a time."

A representative from each team met Boddy in the middle of the field. A coin was tossed, and the Green Team won the right to go first.

"Ah! A preview of our ultimate victory," said a member of the Green Team.

"Don't count your snowballs before they melt," countered a member of the White Team.

"Back to your stations," ordered Boddy as he again ducked behind the tree.

So the team with the green hats threw at the team with the white hats. The white hats threw back, but so far, not one snowball reached its target.

"More snowballs!" shouted Mustard to his teammates. Their pile was almost gone.

"I'm making them as fast as I can," said Plum, who was shivering with cold. "I'm sure my hands have frostbite."

Just then, Plum was hit by the opposing team. Sadly, he sat down. "I'm plum out of this game," he moaned.

"We're winning! We're the best!" shouted a gleeful Peacock as she aimed at Mustard. He dodged, and her snowball sailed harmlessly by. "Not fair!" she protested. "He moved!"

Across from her, wearing fur gloves, Scarlet aimed back at Peacock and threw hard. Scarlet's snowball hit Peacock squarely on the shoulder. "Ha! Take that!"

"How rude!" shouted Peacock, who sat down in

the snow. "That was not nice at all!" She took out a lace handkerchief and blew her nose.

"You're not winning now," taunted Scarlet as she packed several more snowballs.

"That's two gone," observed Boddy.

The two remaining players on each side lobbed more snowballs at each other, huffing and puffing in the cold air.

Finally, a woman with a green hat was hit. "Darn it!" she said, forced to take a seat.

"Ha-ha!" chuckled Plum. "We'll see who has the last laugh."

"Oh, quiet!" grumbled the woman with the green hat. "Your brain is as frozen as your bottom!"

The white team went wild. "Nah, nahnee, nah, nah! You can't hit us!"

The remaining green hat took careful aim at the woman on the other team — and hit her!

"It's down to one against one," observed Boddy.

The snowballs continued to fly as the fallen teammates cheered their remaining partner.

"Come on!" shouted Plum. "Hit him before I freeze to this spot!"

"You can do it," urged Peacock. "But not too hard — we don't want to be rude, even in a snowball fight."

Finally, the white-hatted player hit the other in the back while he was packing snowballs.

Boddy blew the whistle! "That's it!" he bellowed. "The game is won!"

WHO WON THE MATCH? WHO WERE THE PLAYERS ON EACH SIDE?

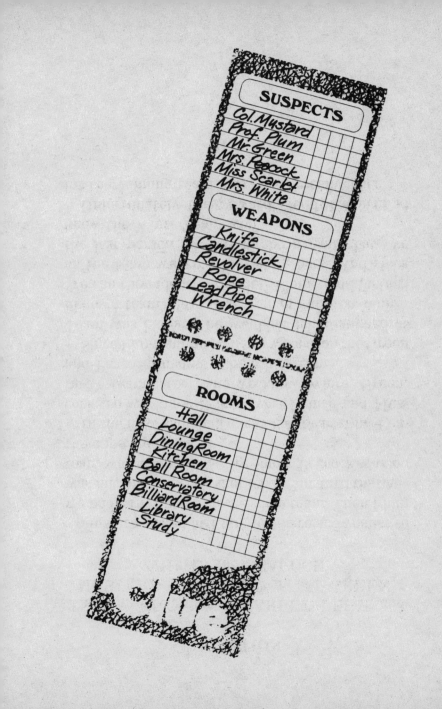

SOLUTION

The White Team won: SCARLET, PLUM, and MUSTARD. The Green Team lost: GREEN, WHITE, and PEACOCK.

Mustard yelled at Plum for more snowballs, so we know they were on the same team. Then Plum was hit, and Peacock shouted at Mustard that her team was winning. So we know Peacock was on the opposite team.

In the next snowball exchange, Scarlet hit Peacock, so we know Scarlet was Plum's and Mustard's teammate. Thus we know White, Green, and Peacock made up the other team.

Since Plum laughed when a woman on the Green Team was hit, and he wouldn't have laughed at his own team's loss, the woman must be White. We can then identify Scarlet, Plum, and Mustard as the team wearing the white hats. And since the last person hit was hit by a white hat, we know the White Team won.

Unfortunately, the "reward" Boddy had in mind for the winning team was — ice-cream cones!

6.
The Case Is All Sewed Up

"MR. BODDY HAS SOMETHING IMPORTANT to show you," Mrs. White told the other guests.

"His last will and testament leaving all his worldly possessions to me?" asked Green.

"His priceless collection of swords, which he's giving to me?" asked Mustard.

"His wonderful assortment of jewels," asked Scarlet, "which he knows will look absolutely gorgeous on an absolutely gorgeous woman like me?"

"His shelf of first-edition etiquette books?" asked Mrs. Peacock.

"Who wants to see us?" asked Plum.

"Please gather in the Conservatory," Mrs. White told them all.

There, Boddy beckoned his guests to a table in the corner where a large patchwork quilt was displayed. "This quilt has been in my family for generations," exclaimed Boddy.

"I'm sure this story will have us in stitches," yawned a bored Mrs. White as she positioned the tea cart near Mr. Boddy's guests.

"Yes," agreed Scarlet, "I'm hanging by a thread."

"Do tell, Boddy," said Mustard gruffly. "We're all on pins and needles."

"Now that you've buttonholed us, Boddy, what's this all about?" asked an impatient Mr. Green.

"I know you get tired of my stories," said Boddy as he gazed fondly at his guests, "but this *is* a good story."

"It better be," Plum complained. "Because I was all ready for bed!"

"This shouldn't take more than a few minutes of your precious time," Boddy said.

"Pour me some tea, please," Mustard asked Mrs. White. "The last time Boddy wanted a few minutes it took all day!"

"I can't begin until you're all settled," Boddy said.

"I hope there's a point to your needling us," replied a peeved Mrs. Peacock.

"There is," Boddy assured her. "Anyway, it all goes back to World War I, when — "

Clunk! Clunk! Getting comfortable, Green took off his shoes and propped his feet on another chair. "Go on," he said.

"It all goes back to World War I," repeated Boddy.

"We already got that far," insisted Scarlet. "Push on!"

Boddy sighed. Sometimes his guests could be so difficult. "It was my great-great-grandmother who — "

"Your granny fought in World War I?" interrupted a confused Plum. "No wonder she was great-great. This *is* a story worth hearing."

"She was not a soldier," corrected Boddy. "Please pay attention."

"It would be easier to pay attention," interrupted Green, "if you paid us."

Ignoring them, Boddy continued, "My great-great-grandmother sewed the family treasures inside the quilt in case the family home was invaded by enemy soldiers."

"Family treasures?" Suddenly Miss Scarlet and the others were very intrigued. "Family treasures? Are they still there?" she asked, moving closer to the quilt.

"Oh, yes," said Boddy, patting the fabric. "Granny used to say, 'A stitch in time saves mine' — or words to that effect."

"What kind of treasure?" asked Green, feeling the quilt for a lump or two.

"Gold?" asked Mustard.

"Coins?" suggested Peacock, eyeing the quilt.

"Jewelry?" asked Plum, wiping his glasses for a closer look.

"Just the typical family treasures," said Boddy.

"Treasures-shmeasures! It just looks like an old

patchwork quilt to me," said a skeptical Mrs. White.

"Looks can be deceiving," admitted a sly Boddy.

"But what are you doing with it?" asked Peacock.

"I'm having it restored by professional seamstresses," Boddy answered. "Look here. And here." He indicated a few places where the fabric was torn.

"You should have asked me for help," said Scarlet. "I sew like a dream."

"Dream on," muttered White. "You just want the treasure."

"That's not true," retorted Scarlet. "I made this very gown I'm wearing."

White examined Scarlet's dress. "I hate to admit it," White admitted, "but Scarlet is, indeed, a fine seamstress."

"She is?" Green asked. "Good. Because I have a pair of trousers I need taken in."

"Then I suggest you 'take them in' to the nearest tailor," replied Scarlet. "I won't sew for anyone but myself."

"Don't worry," said Boddy. "I've hired professional seamstresses to ensure that none of *you* touch this quilt. In fact, from now on, this room is off-limits to everyone except the seamstresses."

"How rude!" protested Peacock. "Banishing us from a room in the mansion!"

"From a room in *my* mansion," Boddy politely reminded her. "You may finish your tea, but then I want you all to stay away until the seamstresses have finished their work."

A half hour later . . .

A half hour later, the last of Boddy's guests finally left the Conservatory. But all afternoon they lurked outside the room, watching as three professional seamstresses mended and reinforced the quilt.

"It makes me crazy that we're outside," one guest complained, "and they're inside near that treasure!"

"Yes, it's a crazy quilt!" joked Mr. Green.

"It really hurts my feelings," protested another guest, "that Boddy would trust outsiders over us. After all, have we ever done the least thing to earn Boddy's suspicion?"

"Well, if someone were to steal the family treasures," another added, "it would be a tailor-made revenge!"

Late that night . . .

Late that night, when the mansion was quiet, a guest sneaked down to the Conservatory. Sure enough, the door was bolted tight.

"Darn that Boddy," the guest muttered. "So mistrusting!"

The guest took out the Lead Pipe and knocked the doorknob clean off the door.

"There, that will show Boddy how to treat his guests," he cackled.

Just as he reached his hand inside to unhook the latch, he was interrupted.

"Too bad you made such a racket, Green," said a voice.

"Oh, it's you!" Green said, squinting in the darkness. "I should've guessed! Well, now that you're here, I suggest that we become partners and — "

Green suffered a blow to the head with a Wrench.

"Sorry," the owner of the Wrench said. "I work best alone." He then unlatched the door and sneaked into the Conservatory.

He felt along the dark wall to locate the light switch.

Just as he found it, though, a Revolver was fired, and he slumped to the floor.

"Too bad, Professor," said the owner of the Revolver. "Next time, think up a better plan."

On the other side of the room, through an open window, a woman in a black mask dropped to the Conservatory floor. As she landed, she lost a small silver object, which went sliding across the floor.

The woman lit a Candlestick and searched for the silver object. "It must be here somewhere . . ." she whispered to herself. "I can't protect myself without it."

In the candle's glow, she saw a figure at work on the quilt. She tiptoed closer.

Out of the darkness, a voice hissed, "Stop! Or I'll shoot you both!"

The two people put their hands up and backed away from the quilt.

Just then, Boddy and White entered the room. "Freeze, all of you!" Boddy cried. "I knew I couldn't trust you!"

"Now, don't jump to conclusions," a male guest said. "Just because you caught us about to rip open the quilt, doesn't mean we were after your treasures."

"That's right," added a female guest. "I came in simply to check the quality of the professional seamstresses' work."

"I don't want your excuses," Boddy said. "And put the gun away, Mustard."

Boddy turned on the light and studied the scene. He carefully examined the quilt. "Drops of blood," he observed. "Someone's opened up my family quilt and was trying to sew it up again."

"Who would do that?" protested a guest.

Then Boddy searched the Conservatory. Under a chair, he found a small, silver object. Holding the object, he approached the masked woman and the other figure who were both near the quilt.

"Let me see your hands," he said.

The two horrified guests showed Boddy their hands.

"I know who did it," Boddy proclaimed. "And this proves it," he added, holding up a small silver thimble. "I know who was tampering with my quilt!"

WHO WAS THE GUILTY PARTY?

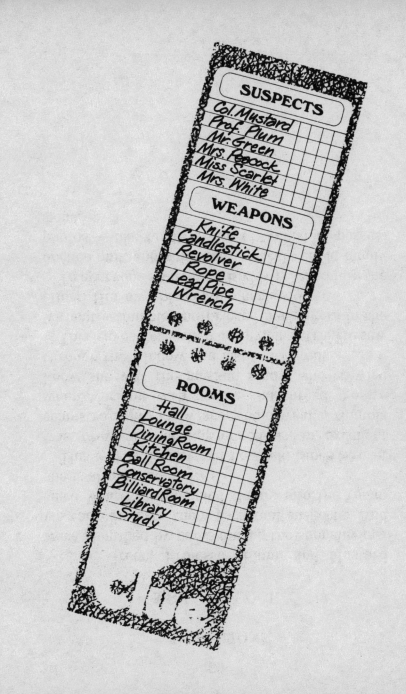

SOLUTION

MRS. PEACOCK

Since Green, Professor Plum, and Mustard were identified by name during the shenanigans, we can eliminate them as actual suspects. And since White accompanied Boddy into the room, she is also eliminated.

This leaves Scarlet and Peacock. Since Scarlet was previously acknowledged as an excellent seamstress, we know she would wear a thimble when working with needle and thread. So we know she was the masked figure who crawled through the window and lost her thimble.

This leaves Peacock, who obviously tried to sew without a thimble and pricked her fingers in the effort. Her own blood gave her away.

To everyone's surprise, Boddy reached into the opened quilt and pulled out a packet of old family photos — his family's most "valuable possessions."

7.
Pie in Your Eye

THE GUESTS HAD GATHERED IN THE Kitchen for a late-night snack of ice cream, cookies, and milk.

"Nothing like milk and cookies to prepare one for a good night's sleep," observed Plum.

"I prefer ice cream," said Scarlet.

"I like both," said Mustard, grabbing another cookie.

As Mrs. White watched them wolf down the snack, she was reminded of something. She got up to check the master calendar, which was always kept on the Kitchen wall.

"I was right," she said, turning to Mr. Boddy. "It's time for your annual Pie Eating Contest."

"Is it really?" asked Mr. Boddy.

"Tomorrow is May fifth — National Pie Day," said Mrs. White.

"Wait a moment," said Professor Plum. "I believe that May fifth is *Cinco de Mayo* — or Mexico's Independence Day."

"Quite right," agreed Boddy. "May fifth is

Cinco de Mayo, and it is also the day I have my contest."

"Don't you remember last year?" asked Mr. Green. "You ate eleven pieces of pie."

"Afraid I don't remember," answered Professor Plum. "But I do hope I enjoyed all that pie."

"I had a stomachache for days," complained Colonel Mustard. "But I was the winner."

"No, you were not," said Miss Scarlet. "I ate twelve pieces — a personal best."

"I will have to challenge you to a duel if you persist in claiming that you were the winner!" thundered Colonel Mustard.

"You're both very rude," huffed Mrs. Peacock.

"No matter how you slice it," said Boddy, "my dear friends always find a reason to argue."

"I say put your mouth where the pie is," said Mrs. White, reaching for her apron.

"Yes, there's only one way to settle this," insisted Mr. Boddy. "Mrs. White, we best start baking."

"But that means staying up all night!" protested White.

"By the time you finish," Miss Scarlet said, arching her eyebrows, "I hope you're 'filling' better."

Mrs. White stormed into the pantry. She returned with a twenty-pound bag of flour.

"I make the best crust in the county," she said, opening the flour bag.

"Yes, it's as flaky as she is," observed Green.

"Watch it," said Mrs. White over her shoulder. "I may just give you a pie in the eye."

The next day . . .

The next day, the guests convened for Boddy's annual Pie Eating Contest. They all sat around the large table in the Dining Room and tucked bibs around their necks.

"Is that your stomach growling?" Green asked Mustard. "Or is a volcano erupting nearby?"

"I purposely went without breakfast and lunch," boasted Mustard, "to leave more room for pie."

"I have plenty of room," said Professor Plum, patting his round belly.

"I may look petite and sweet, but none of you has got me beat!" taunted Miss Scarlet as she pushed in her chair. "I'm ready to take the title once again."

To stop the arguing, Mr. Boddy rang a small silver bell. Mrs. White wheeled in a tray with ten pies, each cut into six pieces.

"Mrs. White, you've outdone yourself," complimented Mr. Boddy. "Please tell us about your wonderful creations."

"This year," she explained with a yawn, "I have two each of five kinds of pie: apple, cherry, chocolate, pecan, and lemon."

"Yum-yum-yum," said the guests, already gripping their forks.

Then Mrs. White put all the pies in the center of the table, each with its own silver pie server.

"When you hear the bell, serve yourself," explained Boddy. "And remember, the person who eats the most slices of pie wins a special memento created just for the occasion."

Then Boddy rang the bell, and the guests went wild.

All except Mrs. Peacock, who sat stiffly in her seat with one piece of apple pie on her plate. "You're not minding your manners!" she said. "You act as if you were born in a barn!"

Ignoring her, Scarlet snatched two slices of each kind.

"You've brought quite an appetite," Plum told her.

"Thank you," she mumbled, her mouth full of pie.

Mustard took one slice of each kind, plus an additional chocolate. "Just for starters," he announced.

"Quit being such a hot dog, Mustard!" scolded Mrs. White.

Green took two slices of cherry and lemon, and three of pecan. "I'm so hungry I could eat a horse," he said.

"Spoken right from the horse's mouth," joked Plum as he took an entire cherry pie, plus two pieces of pecan. "Oh, I'm just nuts about pecan!"

Mrs. White, who was too tired to participate in the contest, cut herself a piece of cherry pie to nibble on while she watched the action. "Ahh, peace at last," she sighed. "At least while I eat this piece."

It was quiet for a few minutes — except for the sound of chewing and swallowing — while everyone devoured their pie.

Then, surprisingly, Mrs. Peacock wiped her mouth daintily and helped herself to another piece — of chocolate. "Just to keep the rest of you company," she explained. "It's only polite."

Mustard stopped eating and groaned. "I can't eat another bite," he said. He put back his two untouched pieces of chocolate.

Plum greedily took one more piece of pecan.

Then Green finished his plate. In a hurry, he reached over to Scarlet's plate and tried to take one of her pieces of pie.

Scarlet screamed and stabbed her fork into his wrist before he could touch her pie. "This will teach you to be greedy, Green!" she sneered.

"Ouch!" He jumped up in pain and knocked an entire apple pie to the floor.

"Now see what you've done!" stormed a furious Mrs. White. "After I slaved all night!" She picked up an entire lemon pie and threw it at Green's face.

"Ahhhh!" screamed Mr. Green. Yellow goo covered his face.

"Mrs. White," ordered Mr. Boddy. "That will be quite enough!"

Everyone had cleaned their plates by then and they all stopped eating to laugh at Green, who was wiping pie from his eye.

"Lemon for an old sourpuss," laughed White.

Before things got totally out of hand, Boddy rang the bell.

"I'm calling an end to this contest right now," he said, disappointed at his guests' behavior.

WHO WAS THE WINNER?
HOW MANY PIECES OF EACH KIND
OF PIE WERE LEFT?

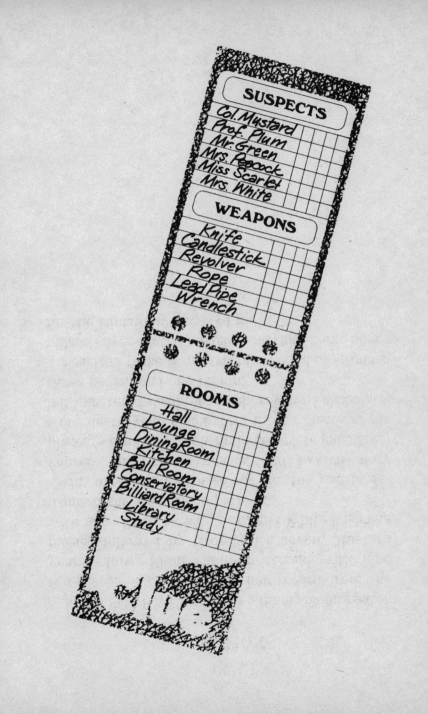

SOLUTION

MISS SCARLET was the winner, having eaten ten pieces — two short of her record from the year before. Plum came in second with nine pieces, followed by Green with seven, Mustard with four, Peacock with two, and White with one (though she wasn't competing).

Out of sixty total pieces of pie, the guests devoured thirty-three pieces, and twelve more pieces (a complete apple and a complete lemon pie) were destroyed. This leaves fifteen pieces of pie left uneaten: two apple; no cherry; nine chocolate; three pecan; and one lemon.

Scarlet's prize consisted of a bottle of stomach pills, a silver-plated pie pan, and take-home boxes for the remaining slices of pie!

8.
Pea Is for Pretender

MR. BODDY AND HIS GUESTS HAD
gathered in the Library after dinner. They were
relaxing, reading, and doing crossword puzzles.

"What's a four-letter word for a stupid person?"
asked Professor Plum, who was stumped.

"Try f-o-o-l," suggested Mrs. White. "I know
several," she added under her breath.

Mustard, reading the newspaper, scanned the
sports section. He put down the paper, disappointed. "Another day without a single duel reported," he said. "What's the world coming to?"

Mrs. Peacock was reviewing a chapter of an
etiquette book. She needed to know how often one
could consult an etiquette book before it was con-
sidered bad manners.

Green borrowed the business section from Mustard's newspaper. "According to this," he said, "I
made four million dollars on my various invest-
ments today. Oh, well, maybe I'll do better tomorrow."

Mrs. White tore out an interesting recipe from

the food section. Discreetly she tucked it in her apron pocket.

Across the room, Miss Scarlet, always the first to become bored, was paging through a dusty old volume of fairy tales.

"Phew," she said, rubbing her nose, "this book is ancient. It smells moldy."

"Ancient and moldy," whispered Mrs. White to herself. "Just like all of these annoying guests my employer keeps inviting."

"Let's see," said Mrs. Peacock, grabbing the book. "Yes, it is moldy," she agreed, wiping her hands on a lace handkerchief. "How rude to leave a rotting old book around. You should toss this in the garbage at once."

"Never!" said Mr. Boddy. He took the book and paged through it fondly. "Why, this was my favorite book as a child. My mother read from it every night before I went to sleep."

"Of course, everyone knows that the old fairy tales are the very root of all literature," said Professor Plum, proud of his knowledge.

"Don't get him started," Mr. Green said with great impatience. "We'll be here all night listening to him go on and on about fairies and dragons and knights in shining armor."

"Well, it beats listening to the stories of your greatest business deals," interrupted Miss Scarlet. "Personally, I always liked the story of the Princess and the Pea."

"The Princess and the what?" asked Mrs. White.

"You know," explained Miss Scarlet. "The princess who was so delicate and sensitive that she could feel a tiny green pea placed underneath thirty-six feather mattresses. I'm just like that myself. So fragile and dainty."

"Ha!" laughed Mrs. White, dusting the old book with her feather duster. "You're so hard-boiled you wouldn't feel a refrigerator underneath your mattress!"

Colonel Mustard stood at attention. "Madam, if you persist in this name calling, I will have to challenge you to a duel."

"I have a better idea," said White. "Let's challenge Scarlet's claim."

"How?" asked Mr. Green.

"I'll go to the kitchen and get a pea," explained Mrs. White. "We'll stack up some mattresses here in the Library and see if Princess Scarlet has a bruise in the morning from lying on a pea."

"An excellent plan," agreed Professor Plum. "Bringing literature alive."

"I don't know about this," said Mr. Boddy. "It seems awful childish."

"So are fairy tales," said Colonel Mustard, pointing at the old book.

"Well, I won't participate in such an unseemly game," announced Mrs. Peacock. She left the room with a dramatic toss of her head.

"Wait!" called Boddy. "It might be fun to see if Scarlet is telling the truth. I've never met a real princess. In fact, if Scarlet turns out to be a real princess, I'll give her a diamond crown from my safe."

"Oh, yes!" breathed Scarlet. "You'll all have to call me Princess Scarlet from now on!"

"Over my dead body," whispered Mrs. White to herself. To the group she smiled and said, "I'll go get the pea."

"Help me bring in some mattresses," Boddy asked the other guests. "We have dozens of extra ones in the attic."

A few minutes later . . .

A few minutes later the guests met back in the Library.

Scarlet had changed into a long dressing gown and carried a fuzzy teddy bear. "I always go to sleep with my bear," she explained.

"A princess with a teddy bear," scoffed Mr. Green. "I don't think so."

"Oh, you'll think so in the morning," said Miss Scarlet. "I may let you polish my crown — if you're lucky."

After clearing the center of the room of furniture, the guests assembled a pile of six mattresses.

74

Miss Scarlet looked at the pile. "How will I get up there?" she asked.

"I'll be happy to throw you," said Green.

"We can use one of the library ladders," suggested Colonel Mustard. "I'll go get one."

"Where is Mrs. White?" asked Boddy. "How long does it take to find one pea?"

"Here I am," Mrs. White said, rushing in. "Sorry, sir. This one was rather resistant to leaving its pod." She showed the guests a single green pea on a silver platter.

"My back hurts already," said Scarlet, "just looking at that awful thing!"

"Pea my guest," said White, grimacing at Scarlet.

Boddy placed the tiny pea underneath the bottom mattress. Then, Colonel Mustard placed the ladder against the mattresses. He gave a gentlemanly hand to Scarlet as she climbed to the top.

"Nighty night," cooed Mr. Green.

"The only pain Scarlet will feel is if she falls off this pile," predicted Colonel Mustard.

From up high, Scarlet arranged herself underneath the blankets and tucked her teddy bear in beside her.

"Sweet dreams," said Mrs. White.

"Let's let Scarlet get her beauty rest," suggested Mr. Boddy.

He was about to turn out the light and close the door when Scarlet let out a scream.

"Ow! I can feel the pea already," she complained. "It feels like a steel beam is piercing my spine!"

"I should have thought of that," joked Mrs. White.

"Liar," said Green to himself. "She just wants the diamond crown. I'll show that trickster."

"Lights out," said Boddy, looking at his watch. "I shall sleep outside the door of the Library to make sure none of you try to, well . . . 'tinker' with the results of the Princess test."

The remaining guests said their good nights, leaving Scarlet — and Teddy — alone atop the pile of mattresses.

Hours later . . .

Hours later, Scarlet was sitting up on the pile of mattresses applying black-and-blue makeup to her leg by the light of a tiny flashlight. "I hope this looks like a bruise," she whispered to herself, dreaming of diamond tiaras.

"You won't get away with it," a voice whispered back, startling Scarlet.

Caught, Scarlet quickly unzipped a secret pocket in her teddy bear and pulled out the Candlestick. With it she clubbed the shadowy figure on the head.

The figure dropped to the floor mumbling, "Fairy tales are the root of all literature."

"I took care of him," Scarlet whispered, continuing to paint her bruise.

"But you didn't take care of me, yet," said a new voice.

Scarlet quickly pulled a Revolver out of her teddy bear and shined her flashlight into the face of the intruder climbing up the mattresses. She then laughed out loud. "Oh, it's only you," she teased. "You'd better leave right now or I'll challenge you to a duel!"

The intruder turned a bright shade of crimson and slinked out of the room in embarrassment. "I hope you get nightmares!" he tossed over a shoulder.

Just as Scarlet was finishing her bruise, she was interrupted again.

"That's the fakest-looking bruise I've ever seen, Princess," said the guest in a high-pitched whine.

"Why, you're no gentleman," hissed Scarlet. "Coming into a lady's chamber in the middle of the night! I'm going to call for Mr. Boddy."

"I wouldn't do that," replied her visitor, pointing the Knife at Scarlet. "I'll tell everyone your bruise is just makeup and you're no princess."

"I'll split all the diamonds in my tiara with you if you promise not to spill the beans — I mean peas," offered Scarlet.

The guest thought for a moment, then said, "It's a deal."

The two shook hands.

"Oh, I can't wait for dawn," trilled an eager Miss Scarlet. "All the loyal subjects will gather around Princess Scarlet!"

WHO CUT A DEAL WITH THE FAKE PRINCESS?"

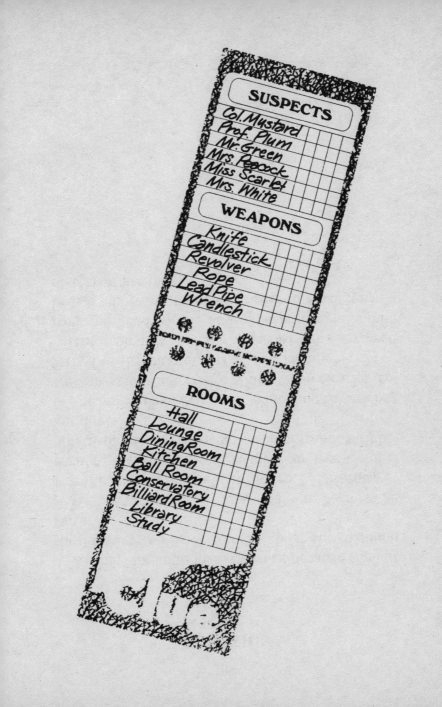

SOLUTION

MR. GREEN

We can eliminate Mrs. Peacock because she left the Library too early to hear about the diamond tiara.

We next eliminate Professor Plum, because he was the guest talking about the "root of literature" earlier. We know the next intruder was Colonel Mustard, because Scarlet teased him about "fighting duels."

The only suspects left are White and Green, but we can safely eliminate White when Scarlet referred to the intruder as a "gentleman."

Unfortunately, when Professor Plum recovered from his head wound and exposed Scarlet's fake bruise, she went from a princess to a pauper in a matter of seconds.

9.
The Thanksgiving Murder

It WAS THANKSGIVING MORNING AT the mansion. Mr. Boddy's guests were enjoying themselves. Green and Mustard were already watching a football game on television. Professor Plum was conducting an experiment on the intelligence of the turkey. Mrs. Peacock and Miss Scarlet were playing gin rummy. When Mr. Boddy invited them into the Billiard Room for a friendly tournament, they all thought it was a splendid idea.

Everyone was having a wonderful time — except for Mrs. White, who was responsible for putting out the holiday meal.

It wasn't long before Mrs. White burst into the Billiard Room.

"I'm glad you're all having such a jolly time playing billiards," she said, "but if you want to eat turkey I must have some help."

"What we should eat is crow," apologized Boddy, straightening up from the billiard table.

"How thoughtless of us. What can we do to help?"

"For starters," said White, "the table needs to be set."

"I'll set the table," Green offered. "If someone else will help me."

"Sometimes you're so helpless," Scarlet told him. "But I'll take pity on you — and help."

"Good," Boddy said. "What else, Mrs. White?"

"I need help stuffing the turkey," answered White. To herself she added, "Before you begin stuffing yourselves."

Peacock volunteered for this task. "I'll do it," she said graciously. "But someone must remember to light the candles. You can't have a nice table without lots of candles."

Colonel Mustard offered his expertise for this chore. "It would give me a glow," he said.

"Then there's the fire to be made in the fireplace in the Library," reminded Mrs. White. "We'll have dessert in there after our dinner."

"I guess that leaves me," said Professor Plum. "I'll fire away!"

"Excellent!" Boddy said. "Everyone is in the proper holiday spirit!"

"Right. Let's get busy," said Mrs. White. "Or you'll have crackers and water for dinner."

"Isn't she the best?" boasted Mr. Boddy. "I should give her a raise."

"I'll raise my glass to that," said Mrs. White.

A few minutes later, Mrs. Peacock was ready to begin her task. She was wearing a pair of elbow length rubber gloves. As she pushed a spoonful of stuffing into the turkey, she hummed to herself. "Over the river and through the woods to grandmother's house we go . . ."

At the oven, Mrs. White checked her pumpkin pies. "Not quite done," she observed. "Well, on to the potatoes."

Scarlet came into the kitchen. "I need one more plate," she said. "I forgot to set a place for Plum. Perhaps because he's always forgetting himself."

"Shouldn't we use nonbreakable plastic for the professor?" asked Mrs. White, reaching in the cabinet.

"No, the table should have uniformity," Mrs. Peacock said, shoving more stuffing into the turkey. "Plastic is not proper for a formal occasion."

While Mrs. White and Mrs. Peacock argued, Scarlet noticed Peacock's valuable jade ring on the table next to where Peacock was working. Apparently Peacock had removed it before putting on the rubber gloves.

"What a beautiful jewel," said Scarlet to herself. "It would look especially beautiful on me."

Pretending she had slipped on something on the

floor, Scarlet bumped into Peacock, sent her spinning, and grabbed the ring.

"So sorry," she said, helping the stunned Mrs. Peacock to her feet.

"How rude! What horrible manners!" spewed Peacock.

"Leave us be," Mrs. White told Scarlet, "before you ruin everything. Here is a place setting for Professor Plum. Now get to work!"

Scarlet curtsied and left.

Smiling to herself, Scarlet returned to the Dining Room with the plates, patting her pocket that held the ring.

As she arranged the salad plates, she happened to see Professor Plum walk through the hallway, carrying an armful of logs for the fire. "Make it a roaring blaze," Scarlet advised.

"Be careful what you tell him," Green told her. "The last time he nearly burned the mansion down."

While Green fiddled with the many forks and spoons, he dropped the Knife to the floor.

"Green, you are so clumsy," Scarlet said. She reached over to pick the Knife up, but as she did, the ring dropped out of her pocket. Scarlet didn't even see it happen.

Mustard, holding a Candlestick in his hand, saw the ring go rolling across the carpet. *Hmm*, he thought. *Don't mind if I do.*

"Pardon me, Miss Scarlet . . ."

"Yes," she replied, turning to Mustard.

Without warning, he hit Scarlet over the head with the Candlestick. She dropped to the floor.

"Ah, you saw the jade ring, too," said Green, picking up the dropped Knife.

"Stand back," Mustard warned, "or I'll thump you, too!"

Green lunged the Knife at Mustard, and the Colonel fled the scene.

"Coward!" Green shouted. "Come back and fight like a man."

"I'm going for help," Mustard hollered over his shoulder. "You won't get away with this."

Mr. Green got down on all fours and crawled on the floor until he found the jade ring. Then he hurried to the door of the Dining Room, determined to find Mustard and keep him quiet.

But just then, another guest met Green at the door and pointed a Revolver at him. "I know your evil little game, Green. Hand over the ring," the guest demanded.

"Okay," agreed Green, not wanting to spend Thanksgiving as dead as the turkey. He handed the ring over to the impatient guest. "By the way," he said, backing away, "you have pumpkin pie all over the back of your hand."

While the guest examined her hand, Green ran from the room.

Wiping her hand clean, the guest then moved over to the windows and held the beautiful ring up to the light.

"I've admired this ring for years," said the woman. "How thankful I am to have acquired it."

"Too bad you don't get to keep it," bellowed a guest from the door, holding the Lead Pipe. "It's mine now."

"No! I won't let you have it."

The pipe-wielding guest grabbed the ring and thwacked the woman.

The last thing the victim remembered before hitting the floor was a face covered with black smudges.

WHO KILLED WHOM AND ENDED UP WITH THE RING?

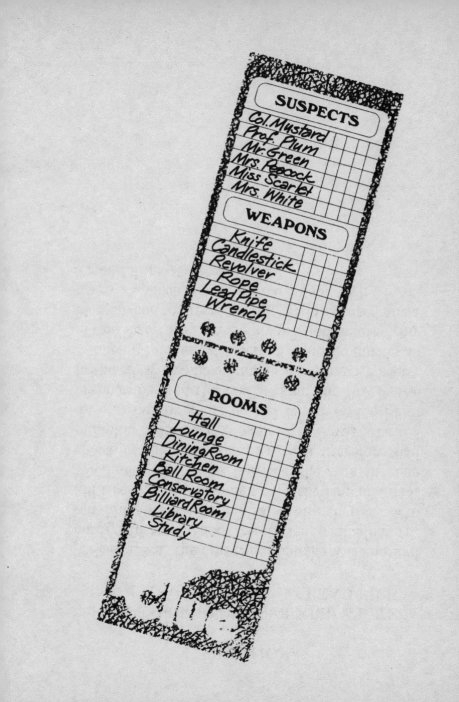

SOLUTION

PROFESSOR PLUM killed MRS. WHITE in the DINING ROOM with the LEAD PIPE.

Scarlet was the first thief, but she was knocked out by Mustard. Then Green tried to kill Mustard, but Mustard escaped. Mrs. White then tried to kill Green, but he handed over the ring and fled. We know it's White because she was the one checking the pumpkin pies, and therefore had pumpkin on her hand. Then White was knocked unconscious by Plum — and we know it's Plum because he was the one making the fire in the fireplace, where he smudged his face with soot.

Luckily, no one was actually injured during all of this chaos. But Mr. Boddy insisted that the ring be returned to Mrs. Peacock, and that each guest make a speech before dinner about "Why I Am Thankful for My Friends."

10.
The Screaming Skeleton

ON THEIR LAST DAY VISITING THE mansion, Mr. Boddy called his guests together in the Library. "Before you leave, I'd like you all to be the first to see the latest addition to my collection of priceless and rare items."

"More coins?" yawned Mrs. Peacock.

"A new painting by a grand old master?" guessed Mr. Green. "That last Leonardo almost put me to sleep."

"No," said Mr. Boddy.

"I know," said Mrs. White. "Jewels."

"No," grinned Mr. Boddy.

"A statue?" guessed Miss Scarlet. "Something marble worth millions with an arm or leg missing?"

"No," said Mr. Boddy. "But you're getting closer."

"We give up," said Professor Plum. "Don't we?"

The guests nodded in boredom.

"Well, then," said Boddy, "take a look at this." He pulled the white sheet off a large object in the corner of the room.

It was a life-size human skeleton.

"How shocking!" said Mrs. Peacock. "It has no clothes on. At least put a pair of gloves on it. Gloves add such a proper touch." She gazed at her own white gloves with satisfaction.

"A skeleton," shuddered Miss Scarlet. "How creepy!"

"Who would want that?" asked Mustard, giving it scarcely a glance. He sat down and began reading his newspaper.

"It's worth millions," said Boddy. "It's made of platinum. I'm donating it to the museum."

"But why platinum?" asked Scarlet as she stepped up for a closer look. "I thought platinum was just for priceless jewelry."

"It will never rust, chip, or tarnish," reported Boddy. "It's one of a kind."

"That's using your 'skull,'" joked Plum as he used the Knife to slice an apple as a snack.

"Oh, you're always 'ribbing' us," added Green.

The telephone in the Hall rang.

"I'll get it," Boddy said. "In my absence, please don't touch my treasure."

No sooner was Boddy gone, than each of the guests began to plot a way to steal the skeleton — or part of it, at least.

Plum approached the skeleton and reached his hand toward the skull. Just as he touched it, it began screaming. A horrible sound! Plum screamed himself and jumped back.

The guests clutched each other in horror.

Hearing the scream, Boddy dashed back into the room. Then, sizing up the situation, he calmly walked over to the skeleton and reached inside the skull.

Soon the noise stopped.

"What was that?" whispered White. She had lost her voice from fright.

"It's a special alarm I had installed," Boddy explained. "I'm the only one who knows how to operate it. You'll excuse me, but with certain guests in the mansion this weekend, I've had to take every precaution."

"You nearly scared me to death!" protested Professor Plum.

"You can look but you can't touch," scolded Boddy.

The guests were daunted by the alarm — but still made plans to try to steal the skeleton.

"If the whole thing is worth millions," said White to herself, "a finger or two would take care of me for the rest of my life."

"Ladies and gentlemen, I know what you're thinking," said Boddy. "But don't waste another moment scheming to steal my skeleton. The museum is picking it up in the morning and paying me in cash."

"Millions of dollars? In cash?" asked Mr. Green. His face was as white as a skeleton should be.

Mr. Boddy politely ignored Mr. Green and ushered everyone out of the Conservatory. He patted his vest pocket, where he had put the key.

He took a final look at his screaming skeleton and locked the door behind him.

"Have you met the people from the museum?" Mrs. Peacock asked. She was waiting quietly in the hallway.

"No, we negotiated the deal through our attorneys," Boddy explained.

"You mean, they wouldn't know you from Adam?" asked Scarlet.

"Or Eve?" added Plum, taking a bite of his apple.

"I'm afraid not," Boddy said. "The arrangements are to leave the money with the person who opens the Library door for them. Who, of course, can only be me."

"Of course," Green muttered, feeling the Revolver in his trouser pocket.

"The key is the key," Scarlet whispered to herself. She opened her purse to make certain she had the Lead Pipe. As a ruse, she removed a compact and touched up her lipstick and blush.

When I get that key, I can be a better Boddy than Boddy, Mustard thought, tightening his grip on the Wrench in the pocket of his hunting jacket.

"I must get my hands on that key," Mrs. White mumbled, taking a Candlestick and proclaiming she must take it to the Kitchen to polish it.

"Don't try anything foolish," warned Boddy.

"As I demonstrated, I've taken every precaution to ensure the safety of my 'friend' in there."

Hearing this, Peacock tested the Rope's strength between her hands.

"We've been warned," smiled Mrs. Peacock.

Several hours later . . .

Several hours later, Boddy waited for the last of the guests to go to bed. Then he turned out the last light in the mansion, checked the locked door one last time, and retired to his room for the night.

No sooner had Boddy closed his bedroom door than a figure carrying the Candlestick descended the stairs, heading for the locked door.

But halfway down the stairs, the person was strangled. The homicidal guest exchanged the murder weapon for the Candlestick.

Using the Candlestick for light, the guest arrived at the door, where another guest waited — holding the Revolver.

"Did you attach the silencer?" the first guest asked.

"Do you think I'm so stupid that I wouldn't?" the offended guest holding the Revolver retorted.

"I think you're so stupid that you *would*. Remember — we need to attract Boddy's attention so he'll come running."

"Right." The guest fired the Revolver, then he and his accomplice hid.

Boddy awoke in his room with a start. "My skeleton!" he cried. He took the key from his vest and dashed downstairs.

But he was in such a panic that he rushed right by a guest lurking outside his room. The guest attacked Boddy with the Wrench and stole the key. Boddy fell on the carpeted floor, moaning.

As soon as this guest reached the top of the stairs, he was hit over the head with the Lead Pipe. "That's what you get for speeding!"

His attacker took the key and dashed down the stairs.

Using the key, the guest opened the locked door and entered.

But before the guest could lock the door from the inside, three other guests rushed in.

"It's mine. Stand back or I'll slice you to pieces!" one guest demanded.

But he was then whacked by the Candlestick. The attacker told everyone else to stand back. "It's mine, now!"

"There's only three of us left," said the guest with the Revolver. "Let's stop this nonsense and split the skeleton — and the money — three ways."

"Fine with me," agreed the guest still holding the Candlestick.

"And me," added the third guest. "Let's shake."

The guest with the Revolver put his hand out —
as did the guest with the Candlestick.

But both were attacked by the guest wielding
the Lead Pipe.

The Revolver and Candlestick fell to the
ground.

Then a major struggle took place. The guest
with the Lead Pipe lost it, but gained the Candlestick.

The guest who had lost the Revolver picked up
the Lead Pipe.

And the guest who had lost the Candlestick
scrambled on the floor until coming up with the
Revolver.

Without warning, a revived Boddy entered the
unlocked Library and turned on the lights.

"Ah-ha!" he shouted, holding his aching head.
"Caught in the act!"

"Ah-ha!" a guest responded. "We have the
weapons!"

The guests forced Boddy to turn off the security
alarm inside the skeleton's skull.

"You'll never get away with this!" a furious
Boddy insisted.

"Oh, really?" a guest mocked.

A shot rang out and Boddy fell dead.

"That wasn't very nice!"

The murderer was given a fatal blow on the
head with the Lead Pipe.

"Good work," the other remaining guest said. "Now the two of us will split the money."

The guest with the Lead Pipe approached the skeleton. "Now we have to make ourselves comfortable and wait for the museum people to arrive with the money."

"No, *I* do," said the other guest, raising the Candlestick and delivering a last, deadly blow.

WHO KILLED MR. BODDY?
WHICH GUEST IS *NOT* DEAD?

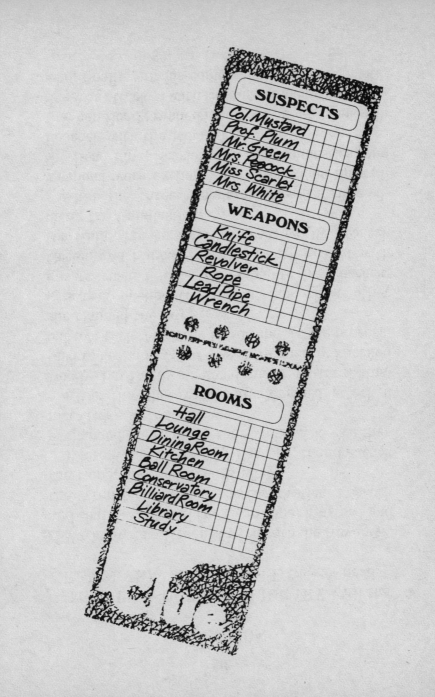

SOLUTION

MRS. PEACOCK in the LIBRARY with the REVOLVER. MISS SCARLET is *not* dead.

We know that Green started with the Revolver, and that Scarlet had the Lead Pipe. Mustard had the Wrench, White had the Candlestick, Peacock the Rope, and Plum the Knife.

White was strangled by Peacock, then Peacock exchanged the Rope for the Candlestick. She then met Green at the Library.

After the shot rang out, Mustard attacked Boddy, but Boddy survived this first attack. Mustard took the key and was subsequently knocked out by Scarlet with the Lead Pipe. In the process, she claimed the key.

Scarlet opened the Library and three other guests rushed in — who have to be Peacock, Green, and Plum. Plum threatened Scarlet with the Knife, but he was then attacked by Peacock using the Candlestick.

After the three remaining guests struggled, weapons were exchanged. Green ended up with the Lead Pipe, Scarlet with the Candlestick, and Peacock with the Revolver.

When Boddy rushed in, he was shot by Peacock. She was attacked with the Lead Pipe by Green — who, finally, got his comeuppance from Scarlet.